Far from our eyes, hidden beneath the crashing waves, King Neptune ruled the great Sea-Kingdom.

Of all his children, his youngest, Princess Leena, was the most curious, especially of the human world above.

Ever since she was a little mermaid, Leena had watched the human ships sailing above. She even had a secret hiding place where she kept treasures that had fallen from some of the ships. Despite her father's warnings, she swam to the surface again and again to see them pass.

"Leena, humans are dangerous!" King Neptune scolded, "I want you to stay away from them!"

One evening, while Leena played on the surface, a ship came into view.

Again disobeying her father, she swam closer until she could hear people talking on the deck.

"It's a beautiful night, Captain," a voice said, "It will be good to get home."

"Aye!" the Captain replied, "Won't be long now, sir."

She could see the men. One held the ship's great wheel, steering a path through the gentle waves. The other was the most handsome man Leena had ever seen! He stood tall and strong, smiling in the sea air. His eyes sparkled like the stars above, and all at once, Leena knew she was in love!

"Your father will be glad to see you," the Captain said, "The King always misses you when you travel."

"The King," thought Leena, "Then he is a ..."

"Yes, Prince Stephan," continued the Captain, "It will be good to be back."

"A prince!" Leena cried, "He's a prince!"

Leena followed behind the ship, watching the prince's every move.

But, someone else was also watching! Cassandra the Sea Witch saw the scene in her crystal ball and smiled wickedly.

"So, the little Princess fancies this human, does she?" the witch cackled, "Well let's see how I can help."

Cassandra pulled some dusty jars off the shelf and poured them into a large black steaming pot. She spoke strange words and stirred round and round. Her eyes grew wide as the spell took effect.

On the waters surface, Leena was so taken with the handsome prince that she did not notice the danger coming until it hit. The Sea Witch had sent a giant wave across the sea. It struck the ship hard, knocking the young prince over the side! The great ship was carried far off into the night, leaving the stunned Stephan thrashing in the cold sea water.

Leena saw the struggling prince slip beneath the waves and swam to his rescue. Diving deep, she pulled Prince Stephan to the surface. Using the last of her strength, she brought him all the way to shore. She kissed him once and said, "I'll see you again, my prince." Then she returned to the sea.

When Prince Stephan awoke, he was alone. He made his way to his father's palace and went inside.

"My boy!" the King shouted, rushing to his son, "I thought you were lost forever!"

"I would have been, father," began Stephan, "There was a girl, a beautiful girl with a voice like music. She pulled me to the beach. I... I don't remember much else." He walked to the window and looked out at the ocean. "Except," he said, "I owe her my life! I must find her and make her my wife."

The King decided to hold a royal ball, and all the young women of the kingdom were invited. Prince Stephan hoped to find his rescuer among the many fair maidens attending.

Meanwhile, back under the sea, Leena sat in her secret hiding place and dreamed about the prince.

"I love him, but how can I ever see him again?"she said sadly, "I wish I had legs instead of this tail!"

Just then, the evil Cassandra appeared. She had been spying on Leena, waiting to do her magic.

"So little mermaid, it's legs you wish for?" she said, "Such an easy request! I can help you... for a price!"

Cassandra told Leena she could cast a spell that would give her legs. But Prince Stephan must marry Leena within a week or the spell would fail and she would be turned into a starfish forever!

"Yes, Cassandra can help you, my dear, and all that I want in return is your beautiful voice!"

"B..But how will I speak to him?" Leena cried, "There is so much I want to tell him."

"A girl can say much without speaking, Princess!" said Cassandra, "You have your grace, your eyes, and your beauty. You need no more." Leena thought, then nodded, "Yes... I'll do it. Cast your spell."

Cassandra gave Leena a potion to drink, then stood back. With a bright flash, Leena's tail melted away, revealing human legs in it's place. Leena tried to speak, but her voice was gone! It was held in a magic blue bubble tied around Cassandra's neck.

"There, there, little one," Cassandra cooed as she swam away, "Remember our bargain!"

Leena came ashore and set off to find Prince Stephan. She came across a sign announcing the ball, and hurried off to the castle. By the time she got there, the party had begun. Music streamed from the castle and the great hall was filled with laughter. Young women from all over came for a chance to dance with the handsome prince and perhaps, to become his bride!

Leena made her way through the crowd until she saw Prince Stephan. He was dancing with a beautiful young woman with dark hair and fiery eyes. "Oh my, that woman looks familiar," Leena thought, but she could not get close enough to be sure.

When the dancing couple waltzed closer, Leena could hear them talking.

"And so, Prince Stephan," the woman was saying, "I found you in the water and pulled you onto the beach. I am the one who saved you!"

Leena wanted to shout, but she could only watch as they glided away across the floor. All night, Leena tried to reach the prince, but the royal guards would not let her near. When the ball ended, the King signaled for quiet.

"Tonight I wish to announce the engagement of Prince Stephan to Lady Sandra," the King said, "I owe her the life of my son and give my blessing to this marriage!"

Leena looked on in horror at the prince and the dark-haired maiden. Then she noticed the strange blue pearl tied around Sandra's neck. But it was not a pearl at all. It was the magic bubble holding Leena's voice! Lady Sandra was really Cassandra the Sea Witch.

"I knew she looked familiar!" Leena thought.

Leena broke through the crowd and dashed up the steps to the throne. She pulled the blue pearl from Cassandra's necklace and crushed it in her hand. At once, Leena's voice flew back into her throat. Sandra changed back into the evil Sea Witch.

"Prince Stephan!" Leena cried, "Look out!"

Cassandra was furious! She screamed, "No, little mermaid. You will not spoil my fun!"

Suddenly Cassandra was holding her crystal ball and began to cast an evil spell. Just then Prince Stephan lunged at the evil Sea Witch and knocked the crystal ball from her hand.

"Fool!" Cassandra shrieked as it shattered on the floor, "You've destroyed me!"

The Sea Witch screamed again as she melted into a puddle of salty water at their feet.

"I told you I would see you again," whispered Leena.
"Your voice! I know that voice," Prince Stephan cried, "It was you who saved me and it is you who I want for my wife."
Leena nodded with tears of joy in her eyes. The King smiled and raised his cup. "A wedding was called for!" he shouted, "And a wedding there shall be!"

And so it was, Princess Leena and Prince Stephan married, and they lived in a castle by the sea.

Sometimes, with the fog low on the water, a sweet mermaid song could be heard drifting across the waves.